THE FOX
AND
THE CAT

THE FOX
AND
THE CAT

Kevin Crossley-Holland's
Animal Tales
from Grimm

Illustrated by Susan Varley

Andersen Press · London

**Translated by Kevin Crossley-Holland and
Susanne Lugert**

First published in Great Britain in 1985 by
Andersen Press Limited,
62-65 Chandos Place, London WC2

British Library Cataloguing in Publication Data

Grimm, Wilhelm
   The fox and the cat.
   1. Tales—Germany
   I. Title II.Grimm, Jacob III. Varley, Susan
   IV. Crossley-Holland, Kevin V. Kinder- und Hausmärchen. *English*
   398′.1′0943   PZ8.1

   ISBN 0-86264-117-9

Colour separated in Switzerland by Photolitho AG Offsetreproduktionen,
Gossau, Zürich

Printed in Great Britain by W.S. Cowell Limited, Ipswich

CONTENTS

Foreword

Jacob and Wilhelm Grimm published their *Kinder- und Hausmärchen* in two volumes in 1812 and 1815. These volumes contain two hundred and ten stories—the greatest body of tales ever collected from oral tradition in the western world.

A number of these folk-tales are set in the animal kingdom. Their heroes and villains are the hare and the hedgehog and bear, the wolf and the fox, the eagle and the wren, the cat and the dog, the donkey and many another. If humans appear in these stories at all, they appear only as supporting cast, and almost always in a bad light! The best of them offer vivid and accurate pictures of animal behaviour and relationships, and at the same time contain sharp lessons for humans about loyalty and disloyalty, kindness and cruelty, the value of family and friends.

It is from these animal tales that we have made our selection. Some of them, like 'The Bremen Town Musicians' and 'The Wolf and the Seven Young Kids' are extremely well-known; others, like 'The Hedge-king and the Bear' and 'The Hare and the Hedgehog' are much less well-known. In making our choice, we have looked for stories that are satisfying in their own right and together make a well-rounded short collection.

As the Grimm brothers moved from house to house, and village to village, recording these tales, they heard many different voices. Some were plain and quite sober, some witty, some rather poetic, some highly idiomatic, some in dialect, though all were matter-of-fact. We have listened carefully to these different strains and hope they can be heard in our translations.

K.C.-H. and S.L.

The Fox and the Cat

It so happened that the cat met Mr Fox in a forest. 'He's intelligent and highly experienced,' she thought, 'and much respected in the world,' and so she greeted him in a friendly way. 'Good day, Mr Fox, old friend. How are you? How are things? How are you getting on in these hard times?'

The fox, who was arrogance itself, inspected the cat from head to foot, and for quite some time he was undecided whether or not to bother to reply. At last he said, 'You shabby whisker-licker, you spotted idiot, you poor scrounger and mouse-hunter, have you gone out of your mind? You dare to ask me how I am? What do you know about life? And how many skills have you acquired?'

'I know only one,' said the cat modestly.

'Well, what is that?' asked the fox.

'When the hounds are after me, I can leap into a tree and save myself.'

'Is that all?' said the fox. 'I'm master of more than a hundred skills and, what's more, I've a sack full of tricks. I feel sorry for you; come with me, I'll teach you how to give hounds the slip.'

While they were talking, a hunter came by with four hounds. The cat leaped nimbly into a tree, and sat up at the top of it where she was completely hidden by branches and leaves.

'Untie the sack, Mr Fox, untie the sack!' the cat called to

him, but the hounds had already seized him and held him fast.

'Well, Mr Fox,' called the cat, 'for all your hundred skills you're stuck. If only you had been able to get up here like me, you wouldn't have lost your life.'

Old Sultan

A farmer once had a faithful dog called Sultan, and he had grown old and lost all his teeth and was no longer able to get a good grip on anything. One day, when the farmer was standing at the door with his wife, he said, 'I'll shoot old Sultan tomorrow. He's no longer any use.'

The woman felt sorry for the loyal creature and replied, 'He has served us well for so many years and been so devoted; surely we should give him food and shelter.'

'Dear me,' said the man, 'you must be mad! He hasn't got a tooth left in his mouth and no thief is going to be afraid of him. He can go! If he's served us well, then he's been paid for it with good food.'

The poor dog, who lay stretched out in the sun not far away, heard every word and was mournful that the next day was to be his last. He had a good friend, the wolf, and that evening he crept out to join him in the forest and complained of the fate that awaited him.

'Listen, old friend,' said the wolf, 'and be of good cheer. I'll help you out of your trouble; I've just had an idea. Very early tomorrow morning your master and his wife are going out to make the hay, and they'll take their baby with them because there's nobody left at home. While they work, they usually put the baby in the shade behind the hedge: you lie down beside it, as if you mean to guard it. Then I'll come out of the forest,

and carry off the baby; you must chase after me for all you're worth, as if you intended to snatch it back from me. I'll let it drop and you take it back again to its parents. Then they'll think you rescued the baby, and be far too grateful to do you any injury; on the contrary, you'll be treated with the greatest honour and they'll never let you lack for anything again.'

This scheme pleased the dog and it was all carried out according to plan. The father yelled when he saw the wolf running across the field with his baby, but when old Sultan brought it back he was delighted; he stroked the dog and said, 'Not so much as a hair on your head shall be harmed, you shall have free food and shelter for as long as you live.'

And the farmer said to his wife, 'Go straight home and bake a loaf and make old Sultan some milksop—he needs no teeth for that. And bring the pillow from my bed, I'll give him that for his bed.' From now on old Sultan was as well off as he could possibly wish.

Soon after this the wolf paid him a visit and was pleased that everything had come off so well. 'But,' he said, 'old friend, you'll wink an eye if I see the chance of carrying off one of your master's fat sheep, won't you! It's getting difficult to win a living nowadays.'

'Don't count on that,' replied the dog. 'I'm still loyal to my master; I couldn't agree to that.'

The wolf, who thought the dog could not have been serious, came slinking up in the dark to carry off the sheep. But the farmer, to whom loyal Sultan had divulged the wolf's plan, was waiting for the wolf and gave him a terrible thrashing with the flail.

The wolf was obliged to run away, but he cried out to the dog, 'You wait, you traitor! You'll pay for this!'

Next morning, the wolf sent the wild boar to challenge the dog to come out into the forest and settle the matter. Old

Sultan could find no second but a cat with three legs and, as they set out together, the poor cat limped along in such pain that it stretched its tail erect in the air.

The wolf and his second were already at the appointed place; but when they saw their opponent approaching, they thought he was bringing a sabre with him—they mistook the raised tail of the cat for one. And as the poor creature hopped along on three legs, they were convinced it was picking up a stone each time and meant to throw it at them. So they both became frightened; the wild boar hid itself in the undergrowth and the wolf leaped onto a tree.

When they drew near, the dog and cat were surprised that there was nobody to be seen. But the wild boar had not been able to hide himself completely in the undergrowth; his ears stuck out. While the cat was having a careful look round, the boar twitched an ear. The cat thought it was a mouse moving there and leaped at it and fiercely bit it. Then the boar gave a great squeal and ran away, calling out, 'Up in the tree! There sits the culprit!'

The dog and the cat looked up and spied the wolf. Then the wolf felt ashamed that he had shown himself so fainthearted, and so he accepted old Sultan's offer of peace.

The Hedge-king

Long, long ago every sound still had its own purpose and meaning. When the smith's hammer rang, it called 'Smite me too!' When the carpenter's plane shaved, it said, 'It's through! It's through!' The mill wheel began to clatter and said, 'Dear God, help me! Dear God, help me!' And if the miller set the mill in motion meaning to cheat someone, the wheel spoke in a most refined way and first asked slowly, 'Who is there? Who is there?' Then it quickly answered, 'The miller! The miller!' And finally, at top speed, 'Brave robber, brave robber, three-sixths from an eighth!'

At this time the birds also had their own language, and everyone understood it. Now it sounds only like a twittering, screeching and whistling or, in the case of a few birds, like music without words.

Now the birds decided that they did not want to do without a ruler any longer and that they would elect one amongst them to be their king. Only one of them, the peewit, was against it: he had lived free and wanted to die free and, anxiously flying to and fro, he called out, 'Where shall I go? Where shall I go?' He retired to lonely, unfrequented marshes and did not show himself amongst his fellows again.

The birds were eager to discuss the matter, and one beautiful May morning they all gathered from the forests and fields, the eagle and the chaffinch, owl and crow, lark and sparrow—why should I name them all? Even the cuckoo came and the hoopoe, his sacristan as he is called, because he is always heard two days before the cuckoo; and a very little bird, who had no name as yet, also mingled with the company.

The hen, who had only heard about the whole business by chance, was astonished at the big assembly.

'What, what is going on here?' she clucked, but the cock reassured his dear wife and said, 'Only rich people,' and then he told her what they had in mind.

It was decided that the king should be the one who was able to fly the highest. When he heard that, the frog sitting in the thicket croaked in warning, 'Not, not, not! Not, not, not!' because he thought this idea would only lead to tears. But the crow said, 'Quark ok,' everything would be settled peaceably.

The birds agreed that they should take advantage of the beautiful morning and set off at once, so that none of them could say afterwards, 'I would have flown even higher, but darkness fell, and I couldn't go on.'

At a given signal, the whole flock soared into the air. Dust kicked up from the fields, there was a great rushing and swishing and beating of wings, and it looked as if a black cloud were passing overhead. But the little birds were soon left behind; they could fly no further and fell back to earth again.

The larger ones lasted longer, but none could rival the eagle, who climbed so high that he could have pecked out the sun's eyes. And when he saw that the others could not keep up with him, the eagle thought, 'Why should you fly yet higher? It's clear enough that you're king,' and he began to wheel down to earth again.

The birds beneath all cried at once, 'You must be our king; none has flown higher than you.'

'Except me,' cried the little fellow without a name, who had concealed himself in the breast feathers of the eagle. And because he was not tired, he climbed and climbed and climbed so high that he could see God sitting on His throne. And when he had completed his ascent, he folded his wings and dropped out of the sky and shouted down in a piercing little voice, 'I'm the king! I'm the king!'

'You our king?' cried the birds angrily. 'You've managed this by cheating and trickery.' So they settled on another plan that the one who was able to delve deepest into the earth should be their king. How the goose slapped her broad breast against the soil! How quickly the cock scratched a hole!

The duck came off the worst: she jumped into a ditch but sprained her ankles, and waddled off to the nearby pond crying, 'What a piece of work! What a piece of work!' But the little bird without a name hunted for a mousehole, crept down it and said in his little voice, 'I'm the king! I'm the king!'

'You our king?' shouted the birds even more angrily. 'Do you think that your tricks will get you anywhere?'

They decided to keep him prisoner in his hole and starve him. The owl was placed as warder in front of the hole and told that she was not to let the little wretch out, on pain of death.

When evening came, the birds were completely worn out after their flight, and went to bed with their wives and

children. The owl stayed alone by the mousehole and looked into it with her great unblinking eyes. After a while, though, she grew tired too, and thought, 'One eye will do; yes, and then you can keep watch with the other one, and the little devil won't get out of his hole!' So she closed one eye and fixed the other on the mousehole.

The little wretch popped his head out, ready to make a getaway, but the owl at once blocked his way, and he withdrew his head again. Then, once more, the owl opened one eye and closed the other; she meant to go on in this way all night long. But when she closed one eye for the next time, she forgot to open the other, and as soon as both eyes were closed, she fell asleep. The little bird soon saw that, and crept away.

From that time on, the owl has no longer let herself be seen by day, otherwise the other birds would chase her and ruffle her feathers. She only flies out at night, and she hates and persecutes mice because they make such horrible holes.

The little bird does not let himself be seen either because he is afraid that he would be in for it if he were caught. He hops around in the hedgerows, and when he feels completely safe, he sometimes calls out, 'I'm the king!' And that is why the other birds mockingly call him the hedge-king.*

But no one was happier that she did not have to obey the hedge-king than the lark. As soon as the sun comes out, she climbs into the sky and cries, 'Ah, how beautiful it is! Beautiful! Beautiful! Ah, how beautiful it is!'

*The hedge-king is the wren.

The Cat and Mouse in Partnership

A cat made the acquaintance of a mouse, and swore such undying love and friendship for her that the mouse finally agreed to share house and housekeeping with her.

'We must lay in provisions for the winter, though,' said the cat, 'otherwise we'll go hungry. You, little mouse, you can't just go wherever you feel inclined or you'll end up in a trap!'

So they took the cat's good advice and bought a pot of dripping. They did not know where to store it, but in the end, after a great deal of thought, the cat said, 'I know no place where it would be safer than the church; no one dares take anything away from there. Let's put it under the altar and not lay a finger on it until we have need of it.'

So the little pot was placed there in sanctuary, but it wasn't long before the cat felt a great craving for it.

'Little mouse,' she said, 'I have to tell you that my cousin has asked me to stand godmother. She has just brought a little son into the world—white with brown spots—and I have to hold him over the font. So let me go out today and leave the house in your safekeeping.'

'Of course,' replied the mouse, 'go in the name of God, and when you taste something good, spare a thought for me; I too would like a little drop of sweet red christening wine.'

But none of this was true; the cat had no cousin and had not been asked to be a godmother. She went straight to the church, sneaked up to the pot of dripping, started to lick and licked off the skin. Then she went for a walk on the roofs of the town, thought things out, and stretched out in the sun;

and whenever she thought of the little pot of dripping, she cleaned her whiskers. She did not return home until evening.

'Ah! You're back again,' said the mouse. 'You must have had a marvellous day.'

'It was all right,' replied the cat.

'So what name has the child been given?' asked the mouse.

'Skin-off,' said the cat very drily.

'Skin-off,' said the mouse. 'That's a strange and peculiar name. Is it common in your family?'

'There's nothing wrong with it,' said the cat. 'It's no worse than Breadcrumb-thief, as your godchildren are called.'

It was not long before the cat was overcome by cravings again. She said to the mouse, 'You must do me a favour and run the house alone again. I have been asked to stand godmother for a second time and, as the child has a white collar round its neck, I can't resist it.'

The good mouse agreed, but the cat sneaked behind the town wall to the church and half-emptied the pot of dripping. 'Nothing tastes quite as good,' she said, 'as something in one's own mouth,' and she was well content with her day's work.

When the cat got home, the mouse asked, 'So what has this child been called?'

'Half-empty,' the cat replied.

'Half-empty! You're teasing me! I've never heard of such a name in my life! I bet it's not in any book.'

Soon after this delicious meal the cat's mouth began to water. 'All good things come in threes,' she said to the mouse. 'I must stand godmother once more. The child is entirely black except for its white paws; apart from them, it hasn't a white hair on its whole body, and that only happens once in a couple of years. So you don't mind if I go out again?'

'Skin-off! Half-empty!' the mouse answered. 'They're such strange names that they make me thoughtful.'

'You,' said the cat, 'sit at home in your dark duffel-coat, with your long plait of hair, and do nothing but mope. That's what comes of not going out during the day.'

While the cat was away, the mouse cleaned and tidied the house, but the sweet-toothed cat licked the pot of dripping clean.

'One can only sleep easy when everything has been cleaned up,' she said to herself, and did not return to the house until after dark, plump and well-satisfied.

The mouse immediately asked what name the third child had been given.

'You probably won't like this one either,' said the cat. 'He is called Quite-empty.'

'Quite-empty!' cried the mouse. 'That's the most suspicious name of all. I've never come across that before. Quite-empty! What does that mean?' She shook her head, curled up and went to sleep.

After that, no one asked the cat to stand godmother again, but when winter had come and there was nothing more to eat outside, the mouse thought of their store and said, 'Come, cat, let's go to our pot of dripping. How good it will taste!'

'All right,' replied the cat. 'You'll enjoy it just as much as sticking your pretty little tongue out of the window.'

They set off, and when they reached the church they found that the pot of dripping was still in its place but that it was empty.

'Oh!' said the mouse. 'Now I see what's been going on. Now it's as plain as daylight what a good friend you are! While you were standing godmother, you've eaten everything: first Skin-off, then Half-empty, then . . . .'

'Shut up!' said the cat. 'One more word and I'll eat you.'

The poor mouse had the words 'Quite-empty' right on her tongue. She had scarcely uttered them before the cat pounced on her, seized her and swallowed her. That's how life is, you see.

The Fox and the Geese

A fox once came across a gaggle of well-fed geese sitting in a meadow. He laughed and said, 'Aha! I've come in the nick of time. You're grouped very nicely so that I can eat you one after the other.'

The geese cackled in terror; they jumped up and began to moan and miserably to beg for their lives.

But the fox would not hear a word of it, and said, 'No! I won't have mercy. You must die.'

At last one goose summoned up her courage and said, 'If we poor geese must really sacrifice our innocent young lives, grant us just one wish: allow us one last prayer, so that we will not die in a state of sin. After that, we promise to stand in a row so that you can take your pick—the fat, the fatter, and the fattest.'

'All right,' said the fox. 'That is fair enough, and it's a pious request: you pray, and for as long as you pray, I'll wait.'

So the first goose began a good long prayer, cackling, 'Ga! Ga!' over and again, and because she showed no sign of coming to an end, the second one did not wait until it was her turn but also began to cackle, 'Ga! Ga!' The third and fourth followed her, and soon they were all cackling together.

(And if they had finished their prayers, there would be more to say, but they are still praying and praying, morning, noon and night.)

The Wolf and the Seven Young Kids

There was once a nanny-goat who had seven young kids and she loved them just as a mother loves her children. One day she wanted to go into the forest to collect food, so she called all seven of them to her and said, 'Dear children, I'm going out into the forest. Be on your guard against the wolf. If he gets in, he'll eat you all, even your skin and bones. The villain often disguises himself, but you will recognise him at once by his gruff voice and by his black feet.'

The kids said, 'Dear mother, we'll take great care. You go and don't worry about us.'

Then the nanny-goat bleated and set off without a worry in her head.

It was not long before someone knocked at the door of the house and said, 'Open the door, dear children, your mother is here and has brought something for each of you.'

But the kids could tell by the gruff voice that it was the wolf. 'We won't open the door,' they cried. 'You're not our mother. She has a lovely gentle voice, but your voice is gruff; you are the wolf.'

Then the wolf went to a grocer and bought himself a large piece of chalk; he ate it and that made his voice gentle. Then he came back, knocked at the door, and cried, 'Open the door, dear children, your mother is here and has brought something for each of you.'

But the wolf had put his black paw on the window-ledge; the children saw it and cried, 'We won't open the door. Our mother hasn't got a black foot like you; you are the wolf.'

Then the wolf ran to a baker and said, 'I have bruised my foot; cover it with dough.' And when the baker had covered it, he ran to the miller and said, 'Sprinkle white flour over my paw.'

'This wolf is up to no good,' thought the miller, and refused.

But the wolf said, 'If you don't, I'll eat you up.' Then the miller was scared and whitened the wolf's paw. Yes, people are like that.

Now the villain went to the door for the third time, knocked and said, 'Open the door for me, children! Your own dear mother has come home and brought something from the forest for each of you.'

The kids cried, 'First show us your foot so that we can tell you are our mother.'

So the wolf put his paw on the window, and when they saw that it was white, the kids believed everything he said and opened the door.

But who came in? It was the wolf. The kids were terrified and tried to hide themselves. One leaped under the table, the second into bed, the third into the stove, the fourth into the kitchen, the fifth into the wardrobe, the sixth under the wash-basin, the seventh into the case of the grandfather clock.

But the wolf plucked them all out and picked them off one by one; he gobbled them up and he gobbled them down; he failed only to find the youngest one, hidden in the clock-case. When the wolf had eaten his fill, he strolled off, lay down under a tree in a green meadow, and fell asleep.

Not long after, the nanny-goat came back home from the forest. Alas, what a sight awaited her! The door of the house hung wide open, the table, chairs and benches were over-turned, the wash-basin lay in pieces, the blanket and pillows were ripped off the bed. The nanny-goat looked for her children but they were nowhere to be found. She called one after another by name, but nobody answered. Finally, when she came to the youngest, a little voice cried, 'Dear mother, I'm tucked into the clock-case.' Then she took out her kid and it told her that the wolf had come and eaten all the others. You can imagine how she wept over her poor children.

At last the nanny-goat left the house, still grieving, and the youngest kid trotted alongside her. When she came to the meadow, the wolf was lying under the tree and snoring so loudly that the leaves trembled.

She walked right round him and saw something was stirring and struggling in his bloated stomach. 'O God,' she thought, 'is it possible that my poor children, whom he gobbled up for his supper, are still alive?'

Then the nanny-goat sent the little kid running to the house to fetch scissors, needle and thread. And then she slit open the monster's belly, and she had barely made the first cut before one kid popped its head out; and as she kept on cutting, all six

jumped out one after the other—they were all still alive and completely unharmed, for in his greed the monster had swallowed them whole.

What joy! They kissed their dear mother, and frisked around like a tailor on his wedding day. But the nanny-goat said, 'Now go and fetch millstones! We need them to fill the stomach of this unscrupulous beast while he is still asleep.'

So the seven kids quickly dragged up the stones and stuffed as many as would fit into the wolf's stomach. Then the nanny-goat sewed him up so that he neither noticed anything nor even stirred.

When the wolf was at last well-rested, he got on to his legs; and because the stones in his belly made him so thirsty, he decided to go to the spring for a drink. But when he began to move, and to sway from paw to paw, the stones in his stomach banged together and rattled. Then he called out:

'What's in my stomach
rumbling and grumbling?
I thought it was six kids;
it's nothing but millstones.'

And when the wolf came to the spring and leaned over the water to drink, the heavy stones dragged him in and he came to a miserable end.

When the seven kids saw that, they ran to the spot and cried out loudly, 'The wolf is dead! The wolf is dead!' And, with their mother, they danced round the spring for joy.

The Fox and the Horse

A farmer once had a loyal horse who had grown old and was no longer able to work. His master did not want to feed him any longer, and told the horse, 'It's obvious enough that I no longer need you, but I mean you no harm. If you can prove you're still strong enough to bring me back a lion, I'll keep you. But now, get out of my stall!'

And with that, the farmer chased the horse off his property.

The horse was sad and made for the forest to find some kind of protection against the elements. There, he ran into the fox, who said, 'Why are you hanging your head? And why are you plodding around on your own?'

'Ah!' replied the horse. 'Greed and loyalty cannot live under the same roof: my master has forgotten how I've worked for him for year after year, and because I can no longer plough properly, he no longer wants to feed me and has chased me away.'

'Without a grain of comfort?' asked the fox.

'Cold comfort,' said the horse. 'He told me that if I'm still strong enough to bring him back a lion, he'll keep me; but he knows well enough that I'm not capable of that.'

'Then I'll help you,' said the fox. 'Just lie down and stretch yourself out and don't move, as if you were dead.'

The horse did as the fox instructed him, and the fox went to the lion, whose lair was not far off, and said, 'There's a dead horse lying over there. Come along with me and you can have a fine meal.'

The lion went with him and, when they were standing by the horse, the fox said, 'This is no place to eat in comfort. I'll tell

you what: I'll tie his tail to you so that you can drag him back into your lair and eat in peace and comfort.'

The lion liked this idea. He positioned himself, and stood quite still so that the fox could secure the horse to him.

The fox, however, used the horse's tail to tie the lion's legs together. He wound the tail around him—a truss so tight and total that no force on earth could have prised it apart.

Now when the fox had tied the last knot, he patted the horse on the shoulder and said, 'Pull, white horse, pull!'

Then all at once the horse leaped up and dragged the lion along behind him.

The lion began to roar so that, from one end of the forest to the other, the birds took to the air in terror. But the horse let him roar! He drew the lion behind him, and dragged him across the field to his master's door.

When his master saw that, he had second thoughts and said to the horse, 'You must stay with me and I'll look after you.' And he gave the horse plenty to eat until he died.

The Hare and the Hedgehog

This story, children, should be taken with a pinch of salt, and yet in the end it is true; my grandfather always used to say (when he found time to tell me this tale), 'In the end it must be true, my son, or else one couldn't tell it.' The story goes like this.

It was a Sunday morning in harvest time, just when the buckwheat was ready and ripe; the bright sun had risen into the heavens, the warm morning wind played over the stubble, larks were singing in the air and bees hummed in the buckwheat fields. People went to church in their Sunday best, and every creature was at peace with himself, including the hedgehog.

Now the hedgehog was standing in front of his door; his arms were crossed and he sampled the morning wind. He hummed a little song just as in tune and out of tune as the way a hedgehog sings on a fine Sunday morning. As he was singing quietly to himself, he suddenly thought that, while his wife was washing and dressing the children, he could take a turn round the field to see how his turnips were coming on. The turnips were in the field next to his home, and he and his family used to take their pick of them; that is why he considered them to be his own.

No sooner said than done! The hedgehog closed the door of the house behind him and set off along the path that led to the

field. He hadn't gone far from the house, and was just on the point of rounding the sloe-bush that lay in front of the field before heading up for the turnip-patch, when he happened to run into the hare who was out and about with similar intentions: namely, to inspect his cabbages.

When the hedgehog saw the hare, he wished him a friendly good morning. But the hare, who was in his way a distinguished gentleman and terribly arrogant into the bargain, did not respond to the hedgehog's greeting but said, sounding as superior as he looked: 'How do you come to be running around the field so early in the morning?'

'I'm going for a stroll,' said the hedgehog.

'A stroll?' said the hare and laughed. 'I think you could put your legs to better use.'

This reply greatly annoyed the hedgehog; he can stand anything but he won't hear a word said against his legs just because nature made them crooked.

'Do you imagine,' said the hedgehog to the hare, 'that your legs are better than mine?'

'That's what I think,' said the hare.

'Let us put it to the test,' said the hedgehog. 'If we raced each other, I bet that I would run faster than you.'

'With your crooked legs! That's laughable,' said the hare. 'All right. Prove it to me if you're so keen about it. What do you bet me?'

'A golden *louis-d'or* and a bottle of brandy,' said the hedgehog.

'Agreed,' said the hare. 'Let's shake on it, and then we can start at once.'

'No, there's not such a hurry,' said the hedgehog. 'I'm still quite empty; I want to go home and have a bit of breakfast. I'll be back here in half an hour.'

With this, the hedgehog went off, for the hare, too, was quite content with this arrangement. While he was on his way, the hedgehog said to himself, 'The hare relies on his long legs, but I'll do for him. He may be a distinguished gentleman, but he's also a stupid fool, and now he will pay for it.'

Now when the hedgehog got home, he said to his wife, 'Wife, get dressed quickly! You must come with me to the nearby field.'

'What's the matter, then?' said his wife.

'I've a bet with the hare for a golden *louis-d'or* and a bottle of brandy. I'm going to race against him, and I need you there too.'

'O my God, husband!' cried the hedgehog's wife. 'Are you mad? Have you lost your wits entirely? How can you hope to race against the hare?'

'Be quiet, wife!' said the hedgehog. 'That's my business. Don't get mixed up in men's affairs. Hurry up, get dressed and come with me.'

What could the hedgehog's wife do? She had to obey whether she liked it or not.

While they were on their way to the field together, the hedgehog said to his wife, 'Now, listen to what I have to say. You see that long field? That's where we'll race against each other. The hare will run in one furrow and I in another, and we'll start from the top end. Now you've to do nothing but stand in the furrow down here, and when the hare reaches this end, you call over to him, "I'm already here."'

By now, they had reached the field; the hedgehog showed his wife where to stand and then went up the field. When he reached the top, he found the hare already there.

'Can we start?' said the hare.

'Certainly,' said the hedgehog. 'Let's get going.'

And with this, each positioned himself in his furrow. The hare counted, 'One, two, three . . .' and raced off at gale force down the field. The hedgehog, however, ran about three steps, then ducked down into the furrow and sat there peacefully.

Now when the hare reached the bottom of the field, running at top speed, the hedgehog's wife called over to him, 'I'm already here.'

The hare drew up and was not a little astonished: he never suspected that it was not the hedgehog himself calling over to him for, everybody knows, the hedgehog's wife looks just like her husband. But the hare thought, 'Something strange is going on here.' He shouted, 'Again! Let's run again!'

Once again he set off at gale force, so that his ears were pinned back against his head. The hedgehog's wife, however, stayed put and unperturbed.

Now when the hare reached the top end, the hedgehog called over to him, 'I'm already here.' But the hare, quite beside himself with fury, yelled, 'Again! Let's run again!'

'It's all right by me,' said the hedgehog. 'I don't mind. As often as you like!'

So the hare ran another seventy-three times and the hedgehog always held his own with him. Whenever the hare reached the top or the bottom, the hedgehog or his wife said, 'I'm already here.'

But the hare could not finish the course for the seventy-fourth time. He collapsed in the middle of the field, blood streamed from his throat, and he died in that very place.

The hedgehog, however, took his winnings—the golden *louis-d'or* and the bottle of brandy. He shouted to his wife to come out of the furrow, and they cheerfully went home together; and if they aren't dead, they are still alive.

So it was that on Buxtehude Heath the hedgehog ran the hare to death; and since that time, no hare has had the least wish to race against the Buxtehude hedgehog.

The morals of this story are that, firstly, no one—however distinguished he thinks himself to be—should dare to make fun of lesser men, not even the hedgehog. And secondly, when someone marries, I suggest that he should take a wife of his own kind, and one who looks just the same as he does. So, whoever is a hedgehog must see to it that his wife is a hedgehog too, and so on.

The Wolf and the Fox

The fox was the wolf's companion; he had to do whatever the wolf desired, because he was the weaker, and he would have liked to get rid of his master.

One day they were walking through the forest together when the wolf said, 'Red fox, find me something to eat, or else I'll eat you.'

'I know a farm where there are a couple of baby lambs,' replied the fox. 'Shall we go and get one?'

The wolf liked this idea, so they went to the farm and the fox stole the baby lamb, brought it to the wolf, and then made off.

Then the wolf ate it but he still was not satisfied; he wanted to have the other one too, and went back to get it. Because the wolf was so clumsy, the baby lamb's mother caught him in the act, and started wailing and bleating so that the farmer and his family came running to the spot. They found the wolf there and gave him such a beating that he limped back to the fox, howling.

'You've well and truly tricked me,' said the wolf. 'I wanted to get the other lamb, and the farmer and his family caught me and beat me into pulp.'

'Why are you such a glutton?' the fox replied.

The next day they went walking again, and once more the

greedy wolf said, 'Red fox, find me something to eat, or else I'll eat you.'

'I know a farmhouse where the farmer's wife is making pancakes tonight,' the fox replied. 'Let's go and get some.'

Off they went and the fox sneaked round the house, peeping and sniffing until he discovered the pancake bowl; then he peeled away six pancakes and brought them to the wolf. 'Here's something for you to eat,' he said to the wolf, and made off.

The wolf swallowed the pancakes in one mouthful. 'Very tasty!' he said, and he went and pulled down the bowl so that it smashed into pieces. That made such a terrible clatter that the farmer's wife came in, and when she saw the wolf, she called for everyone. They came at the double and beat the wolf, they beat him black and blue so that he hobbled back to the fox in the forest with two lame legs, howling loudly.

'What a nasty trick to play on me!' said the wolf. 'The farmer's wife and her family caught me and gave me a good thrashing.'

But the fox only said, 'Why are you such a glutton?'

On the third day, they went out together and the wolf could only limp along painfully; nevertheless, he said once again, 'Red fox, find me something to eat, or else I'll eat you.'

'I know a man who has just killed an animal, and the salted meat lies in a barrel in the cellar,' replied the fox. 'Let's go and get it.'

'I'll go with you at once,' said the wolf, 'and you can help me if I'm unable to get away.'

'All right,' said the fox, and he showed him the tricks and dodges which enabled them at last to get into the cellar.

There was meat by the joint there, and the wolf set about it at once, and thought, 'I'm going to take my time over this.'

The fox tucked in, too. He kept glancing around, and often ran back to the hole through which they had come to test whether his body was still slim enough to slip through.

'Tell me, dear fox,' said the wolf, 'why do you keep running to and fro, and jumping in and out?'

'I'm just checking that nobody is coming,' said the crafty one. 'Don't eat too much.'

'I'm staying here until this barrel is empty,' said the wolf.

Meanwhile the farmer, who had heard the noise of the fox leaping about, came into the cellar. When the fox saw him, he disappeared through the hole in one leap; the wolf tried to follow him but he was now so barrel-chested that he could no longer slip through, but got stuck.

Then the farmer fell on him with a cudgel and beat him to death. But the fox leaped into the forest and was delighted to have got rid of the old glutton.

The Hedge-king and the Bear

One summer day the bear and the wolf were walking in the forest when the bear heard the most beautiful birdsong.

'Brother wolf,' he said, 'what bird is that singing so beautifully?'

'That's the king of the birds,' said the wolf. 'We all have to bow down before him.' But it was only the hedge-king.

'If that's the case,' said the bear, 'I'd like to have a look at his royal palace; come and show me the way.'

'It's not as simple as that,' said the wolf. 'You'll have to wait until the queen gets back.'

Soon afterwards, the queen arrived with food in her beak, and so did the king, to feed their chicks. The bear would have liked to follow them there and then, but the wolf tugged at his sleeve and said, 'No, you must wait until the king and queen have gone away again.'

So they kept an eye on the hole where the nest was, and then they went for a stroll. But the bear was restless: he wanted to see the palace and after a short while went back to the hole.

The king and the queen had really left the nest now. The bear peered into the hole and saw five or six chicks lying in it. 'Is this the royal palace?' cried the bear. 'It's a miserable palace! And you're not princes and princessess, you're deceitful children.'

When the little hedge-kings heard that, they flew into a terrible rage and cried, 'No, we're not, our parents are honest people. Bear, we're going to get even with you for this.'

The bear and the wolf were anxious; they made off and gloomed in their lairs. But the little hedge-kings went on shouting and screaming, and when their parents came back with food, they said, 'We won't touch a fly! Not even a tiny leg! Unless it's decided whether or not we're honest children, we'll starve to death. The bear has been here and insulted us.'

Then the old king said, 'Keep calm, everything will be put right.'

He flew off with his queen to the bear's lair and shouted in, 'Why have you insulted our children, you old growler? You're going to have to pay for this; we'll settle this in a fight to the finish.'

So war was declared on the bear and he summoned all the four-footed beasts: the ox, the donkey, the cow, the stag, the deer, and everything else that walks on earth.

But the hedge-king summoned everything that flies in the air: not only the big and small birds, but also the gnats, hornets, bees and flies were called into action.

Now when the time of the battle drew near, the hedge-king sent out scouts to find out who was Commander-in-Chief of the enemy. The gnats were the most cunning of all; they swarmed into the forest where the enemy was drawing up, and one finally settled under a leaf of the very tree where the orders were being handed down.

The bear was standing there. He called the fox to him and said, 'Fox, you're the most cunning of all the animals. You must be general and lead us.'

'All right,' said the fox. 'So what shall we take as the signal to begin?'

Nobody was able to think of anything.

'I have a beautiful long bushy tail,' said the fox, 'and it looks much the same as a plume of red feathers. When I hold up my tail, our chances will be good and you must advance; but if I let it drop, then take to your heels.'

When the gnat heard that, she flew back and disclosed every scrap of information to the hedge-king.

When the day of the battle dawned—Oh! then the four-footed beasts came pounding along to the battlefield so that the earth trembled; and the hedge-king and his army converged on that place through the air so that it purred and cried and whirred, and struck fear and terror into the heart. And so both sides attacked one another.

Then the hedge-king despatched the hornets with orders to sit under the fox's tail and sting him for all they were worth. Now when the fox was stung for the first time, he winced and raised one leg, but he bore the pain and went on holding his tail erect; at the second sting, he had to drop it for a moment; but at the third sting, he could no longer bear the pain, cried out and let his tail fall between his legs. When the animals saw that, they thought that all was lost and took to their heels, each to his own lair; and so the birds had won the battle.

Then the king and the queen flew home to their children and called out, 'Be happy, children. Eat and drink to your hearts' content; we have won the war.'

'No, we won't eat yet,' said the little hedge-kings. 'First the bear must come to our nest and ask for our forgiveness and say that we are honest children.'

So the hedge-king flew to the bear's den and called out, 'You must come to the nest, growler, and beg my children's forgiveness, and tell them that they are honest children, otherwise we'll smash every rib in your body.'

Hearing this, the bear dragged himself along in utter terror and begged for forgiveness. Only now were the little hedge-kings satisfied. They sat themselves down, and ate and drank and made merry until late that night.

The Bremen Town Musicians

A man once had a donkey who had patiently carried sacks to the mill for years and years, but the donkey was worn out and able to do less and less work. Then his master decided to stop feeding him. The donkey, though, knew that something was in the wind, so he ran away, and set out for Bremen: there, he thought, he could become a town musician.

When he had walked for a while, the donkey came across a hound, lying by the roadside, who was panting like someone who had run for miles and miles. 'Why are you panting like that, snapper?' asked the donkey.

'Alas!' said the hound. 'Because I am old and growing weaker each day, and can't go hunting any longer, my master wanted to kill me, and so I've run away. But now, how can I make my living?'

'I've an idea,' said the donkey. 'I'm going to Bremen to be a town musician. Come with me and you can be a musician too. I'll play the flute and you can beat the kettle-drum.'

The hound was well pleased, and they set off together. It wasn't long before they came across a cat sitting on the road and pulling a face as long as a month of Sundays.

'Now what's wrong with you, old whisker-licker?' said the donkey.

'Who can be happy when he is in for it?' replied the cat.

'Because I'm old, and my teeth are blunt and I prefer not to hunt mice but sit behind the stove and spin, my mistress wanted to drown me. I had a narrow escape, but now I need some good advice: where shall I go?'

'Come with us to Bremen. You know a thing or two about night-music, and you can become a town-musician there.'

The cat liked this idea and set off with them. Then the three refugees passed by a farm where a cock was sitting on the gate and crowing to high heaven.

'That sound sends a chill to the marrow-bone,' said the donkey. 'What's the reason for it?'

'I've prophesied good weather,' said the rooster, 'because it is Lady Day; Mary has washed the Christ child's swaddling clothes and wants to dry them. But because it is Sunday tomorrow and we have guests, the mistress of the house won't spare me. She has told the cook that she wants chicken-stew tomorrow, and so I am going to lose my head tonight. Now I'm crowing for all I'm worth while I still can.'

'Fiddlesticks, redhead!' said the donkey. 'You would do better to come along with us. We're going to Bremen, and you'll find something better than death wherever you go.

You've a fine voice, and when we all make music together, we should make a good sound.'

The rooster liked this idea, and all four of them set off together. They were unable, though, to reach the town of Bremen in one day and that evening they came to a forest where they thought they would spend the night. The donkey and the hound lay down under a big tree, and the cat and the rooster made for the branches, but the rooster flew to the top of the tree—the safest place for him. Before he went to sleep, he looked around in all four directions, and then he thought he could make out a light burning in the distance. He called out to his companions that there must be a house not far away because a light was shining.

'It's pretty poor shelter here,' said the donkey. 'So let's get up and head for it, late as it is.'

The hound said that he could do with a couple of bones into the bargain, with some meat on them. So they set off in the direction of the light. They soon saw it gleaming more brightly, and it got bigger from moment to moment, until they were standing in front of a brightly-lit thieves' kitchen.

Being the largest, the donkey edged up to the window and peered in.

'What can you see, greyhair?' asked the rooster.

'What can I see?' replied the donkey. 'A table laden with good things to eat and drink and robbers sitting around it enjoying themselves.'

'Just the thing for us,' said the rooster.

'Yes, yes,' said the donkey. 'Ee-aw! If only we were in there.'

Then the animals discussed how they could manage to chase away the robbers, and at last they hit upon an idea. The donkey had to plant his forelegs on the window-ledge, the hound had to jump on to the donkey's back, and the cat had to scramble on to the hound, and finally the cock flew up and

perched on the head of the cat. When they had done this, at a given signal they all began to make their music together; the donkey brayed, the hound barked, the cat miaowed, the cock crowed; then they launched themselves through the window into the kitchen, so that the panes were shattered.

The robbers leaped up at this appalling hullaballoo. They were quite convinced that a ghost had come in, and fled to the forest in complete and utter terror. And the four companions sat down at the table, and contented themselves with what was left over; they ate as if they were about to fast for the next four weeks.

When the four minstrels had finished, they extinguished the light and looked for a good place to sleep, each according to his nature and inclination. The donkey lay down on the dunghill, the hound behind the door, the cat on the stove by the glowing embers, and the rooster perched on the rafters; and because they were tired after their long journey, they soon fell asleep.

After midnight the robbers saw from a distance that there was no longer a light burning in the house, and everything seemed to be quiet. 'We shouldn't have been scared out of our wits,' said their chief, and he instructed one of his men to go and inspect the house. This man found everything quiet. He went into the kitchen to prime the lamp, and because he took the glowing, fiery eyes of the cat to be burning coals, he held out a taper so as to light it.

But the cat did not see the joke and sprang at his face, spitting and scratching. Then the man was scared to death; he bolted for the back door, but the hound lying there leaped up and bit his leg; and as he ran across the yard past the dunghill, the donkey gave him the devil of a kick with his hindleg; and the rooster, who had been disturbed by this racket and was now fully awake, shouted down from his rafter, 'Kikeriki!'

The robber ran back to his chief as fast as he could and said, 'Oh! There's a frightful witch in the house. She breathed all over me and scratched my face with her long fingers; and standing in front of the door, there is a man with a knife who stabbed me in the leg; and lying in the yard there is a black monster who attacked me with a cudgel; and up in the rafters sits a judge who shouts, "Bring the rogue here to me." So then I made off as fast as I could.'

From then on, the robbers no longer dared to go into the house, and the four Bremen musicians felt so comfortable there that they had no wish to leave the place again. And whoever told this story last still has a warm mouth.